Oh, Cats!

by Nola Buck
pictures by Nadine Bernard Westcott

HarperTrophy®
A Division of HarperCollins*Publishers*

HarperCollins®, ☝®, Harper Trophy®, and I Can Read Book®
are trademarks of HarperCollins Publishers, Inc.

Oh, Cats!
Text copyright © 1997 by Nola Buck
Illustrations copyright © 1997 by Nadine Bernard Westcott, Inc.
Printed in the U.S.A. All rights reserved.

Library of Congress Cataloging-in-Publication Data
Buck, Nola.
  Oh, cats! / by Nola Buck; illustrated by Nadine Bernard Westcott.
    p.   cm. — (A my first I can read book)
  Summary: A child plays with three new cat friends.
  ISBN 0-06-025373-8. — ISBN 0-06-025374-6 (lib. bdg.)
  ISBN 0-06-444240-3 (pbk.)
  [1. Cats—Fiction.   2. Stories in rhyme.]   I. Title.   II. Series.
PZ8.3.B846Oh   1997   95-10129
[E]—dc20   CIP
                                                                    AC

First Harper Trophy edition, 1998
❖
Visit us on the World Wide Web!
http://www.harperchildrens.com

For Becky

(and her cat friends, Gussie and Woody)

I can see cats.

One, two, three cats.

I can say cats.

Come and play, cats.

Up you go, cats.

No, no, no, cats.

Where are you, cats?

I see two cats.

I will come, cats,
to find one cat.

Now I see cats.

One, two, three cats.

You come down, cats.

Come down now, cats.

Jump and play, cats.

16

Run away, cats?

No, no, no, cats.

Do not go, cats.

If you stay, cats,
we will play, cats.

Up to you, cats.

Be my new cats.

Like you so, cats . . .

Oh, cats!